Minsha's Night on Ellis Island

Also by Pam Berkman and Dorothy Hearst

Filigree's Midnight Ride

Bo-Bo's Cave of Gold

Minsha's Night on Ellis Island

Pam Berkman and Dorothy Hearst

Illustrated by Claire Powell

Margaret K. McElderry Books

New York London Toronto Sydney New Delhi

MARGARET K. McELDERRY BOOKS

An imprint of Simon & Schuster Children's Publishing Division

1230 Avenue of the Americas, New York, New York 10020

MARGARET K. McELDERRY BOOKS is a trademark of Simon & Schuster, Inc.

For information about special discounts for bulk purchases, please contact Simon & Schuster Special Sales at 1-866-506-1949 or business@simonandschuster.com.

The Simon & Schuster Speakers Bureau can bring authors to your live event. For more information or to book an event, contact the Simon & Schuster Speakers Bureau at 1-866-248-3049 or visit our website at www.simonspeakers.com.

Also available in a Margaret K. McElderry Books paperback edition

Book design by Debra Sfetsios-Conover and Rebecca Syracuse

The text for this book was set in Caslon Old Face BT.

Cover art for this book was rendered by hand and colored in Photoshop. All interior illustrations have been drawn by hand using pencil and graphite.

Manufactured in the United States of America

0720 RR4

First Margaret K. McElderry Books hardcover edition August 2020

2 4 6 8 10 9 7 5 3 1

Library of Congress Cataloging-in-Publication Data

Names: Berkman, Pamela, author. | Hearst, Dorothy, author. | Powell, Claire, illustrator.

Title: Minsha's night on Ellis Island / Pam Berkman and Dorothy Hearst ; illustrated by Claire Powell.

Description: First edition. | New York : Margaret K. McElderry Books, [2020] | Series: At the heels of history | Audience: Ages 6–9. | Audience: Grades 2–3. | Summary: Separated from her family when they leave Beirut for America in 1921, Minsha the terrier befriends Yusef and faces challenges while helping him reunite with his family before seeking her own. Includes historical notes.

Identifiers: LCCN 2019039464 (print) | ISBN 9781534433380 (paperback) | ISBN 9781534433397 (hardcover) | ISBN 9781534433403 (eBook)

Subjects: CYAC: Emigration and immigration—Fiction. | Terriers—Fiction. | Dogs—Fiction. | Ellis Island Immigration Station (N.Y. and N.J.)—Fiction. | Family—Fiction.

Classification: LCC PZ7.1.B457 Min 2020 (print)

LC record available at https://lccn.loc.gov/2019039464

To the twelve million men, women, and children who left behind everything they knew to cross the registry room at Ellis Island, and to the many thousands making similar journeys today.

P. B. and D. H.

1

The Ship to America

1921, Port of Beirut, Greater Syria

Minsha barked and barked as she watched the big steamship chug out to sea. She pulled hard against her collar. But Uncle Sami held tight.

"Let me go!" Minsha woofed.

"Sorry, girl," Uncle Sami said, almost as if he could understand her. "They don't allow dogs on those ships to America! You'll stay with me now."

Minsha didn't care what was allowed. Leila was on that ship. Minsha had to get to her.

"I need to catch that ship!" she woofed.

Uncle Sami was kind. But he didn't throw his arms around Minsha the way Leila did. Or play tug-a-rag after supper. Or pull gently on Minsha's big, pointy ears. Leila was Minsha's family. Minsha had never belonged to anyone else. She hadn't been able to believe it when Leila's parents said they were all going to America and leaving Minsha behind.

They lived on a farm near the foot of Mount Lebanon. Before the war they sometimes went to Beirut to visit Uncle Sami. The family always went home together. But not this time.

"We can't leave without Minsha!" Leila had cried to her parents. She'd thrown her arms tightly around Minsha, her eyes flashing. "We're family! We stick together and help each other! We don't leave anyone behind!"

Minsha had woofed in agreement.

But Minsha

was a dog and Leila was only nine years old. They didn't get to decide anything.

"That's enough," Leila's father had said. "We don't have any choice. She can't come with us and we have to leave. There's been so much fighting, and there isn't enough food. No one has money to buy what we grow. We can start again in New York City."

He had taken Leila's arm and dragged her away while Uncle Sami held tight to Minsha's collar. The family got on one of the small boats that were tied up at the harbor. The boat took them out to a big ship. Now the big ship was moving farther and farther away. Minsha's heart felt like something was squeezing it tight.

She pulled harder. Uncle Sami didn't know her tricks like Leila did. He loosened his grip for a moment. Minsha lowered her head and twisted her shoulder at the same time. Uncle Sami tried to grab her, but her smooth fur made it hard for him to hold on. She broke free and raced toward the docks.

Minsha was a good swimmer. She felt sure she could make it to the ship before it was too far away. Then Leila's parents would have to take her with them to America.

"Minsha!" called Uncle Sami.

She ran faster. "Get out of my way!" she barked to the people who crowded the port. She dodged a shiny automobile.

She made it onto the dock. She was just about to leap into the water when something knocked her over.

A tough-looking dog stared down at her. He looked like the dogs back home who didn't have families of their own.

"That's a bad idea," the dog said. "Those ships move fast. You'd drown before you got anywhere near it."

Minsha scrambled to her paws. "You shouldn't have stopped me!" she barked. "My family is on that ship!" It was getting farther and farther away on the endless gray sea.

"That's tough luck," the other dog said. "Half the salt water in this bay comes from the tears of people who get left behind." He sat down. "Everyone's going to America. I hear things are good there. But I think there's probably good and bad there, like everywhere else."

"I'll follow them!" Minsha howled.

The dog snorted. "It takes a *steamship* almost three weeks to get to America. You think you can keep up?" Minsha knew the other dog was right. The ship was moving faster than any dog could swim.

The dog looked Minsha up and down. "You'd be handy in our pack. You're a terrier—the kind that catches rats, right? You can stay in Beirut with us. I can tell you where to get a sausage. We'll help you settle in. We have a nice little family here."

Minsha's fur bristled. "I *have* a family, and I don't need a sausage," she said. "I need my girl, Leila."

"Fine," said the dog, getting up to trot away. After a few steps he stopped. "There'll be another ship leaving same time tomorrow," he said over his shoulder. "From this pier. It's going to the same place, New York City. In America. You can get on the little boats and then hop onto the big ship."

Minsha was sorry she'd snapped at the dog. "Thank you," she said.

"Want to sleep with us in back of the big

souk tonight?" asked the dog. "People throw out really good bones there."

"No, I'll stay here," Minsha answered. "I don't want to miss that boat."

The dog sighed and headed up the waterfront.

Minsha heard Uncle Sami calling and calling. She hid behind a tall pile of grain sacks. She watched the ship Leila was on until it was out of sight.

2
Stowaway Dog

The next morning, Minsha woke up before the sun rose. She ran to the little boats at the water's edge. She made sure no one was looking. Then she put her front paws on the edge of one of the boats. She pushed off with her back legs and tumbled in. She looked for a place to hide and saw a tarp that was stretched over the back of the deck. She crawled under it. She sat down on something hard. It felt like a rock.

"Get off me," the rock said.

Minsha jumped to her paws.

A turtle blinked up at her.

"Sorry," Minsha said to him. "Can you tell me if this boat goes to the big ship to America?"

"Yes," the turtle said slowly. He closed his eyes and drew his head into his shell.

Minsha stayed perfectly still. She hid as people climbed aboard. The boat bobbed over the water. When it stopped moving, she poked her head out from under the tarp.

"Hey!" a man yelled. "Whose dog is this? Get it off!"

He tried to pick her up.

"Hands off!" barked Minsha.

She shot like lightning past his hands.

"So *fast*," she heard the turtle mutter. "Boats are like stepping stones, fast dog."

Stepping stones! Of course! Like the

stones that Minsha and Leila used when they crossed the stream back home.

Other boats floated all around Minsha, almost touching. She jumped to the nearest one and then the next. She hopped from one boat to another until a huge metal wall rose above her like a cliff. It was the side of the steamship. It looked as big as Mount Lebanon itself.

She teetered on the small boat's edge.

Stairs led up the side of the ship. There was a gap between Minsha's boat and the stairs. She looked down into the deep, dark water. Then she jumped.

She made it! She ran up the stairs and was almost on the ship when a pair of large feet blocked her way. She looked up.

A big sailor stood at the top of the stairs.

"Hey!" he shouted. "No dogs allowed!" He planted his feet wide apart and bent down. He reached out his arms to grab Minsha.

Minsha dove between his legs. She bolted across the deck. It was crowded with people. They bustled to different parts of the ship with their bags and bundles and trunks. All around her stood strange equipment that smelled like metal and coal.

"Someone throw that dog over the side!" the sailor bellowed.

Minsha saw a big square hole in the deck. What looked like hundreds of passengers were walking into it and down metal steps. The stairs clanked and clanged under their feet.

Minsha knew she had to stay hidden. She dove straight into the crowd and followed them. She squeezed between knees and bags and feet, trying not to trip anyone.

At the bottom of the stairs was a huge room with curved walls. There were some bunk beds stacked three tall. The room moved back and forth and back and forth. It made Minsha's stomach feel strange.

Minsha had never seen so many people crammed into one place. They spoke using all sorts of different words. Minsha had learned that people from different places often couldn't understand one another. She was glad dogs didn't have that problem.

At first, no one noticed her. Then a boy putting a suitcase up on a bunk looked right at her. She was caught!

The boy smiled at her. He was about the same age as Leila. His eyes and hair were dark. A small girl standing next to him put her finger to her lips. An even smaller boy waved.

A woman standing next to the older boy put her hand on his shoulder.

"Hurry with that, Yusef," she said. She sounded tired. "I need you to watch over your brothers and sisters."

"Yes, Mama," the boy named Yusef said. "Don't worry. I'll take care of them." He pulled a very small girl out from under a big rolled-up rug.

"Where did that dog go?" a voice boomed. The sailor who had tried to catch Minsha stomped down the stairs behind her.

The boy was still watching her. He gestured "come" to Minsha.

Minsha didn't know if she could trust him. He wasn't family. But she couldn't get thrown off the ship.

Minsha darted to the boy.

"Shhh, doggy," said the girl.

The boy leaned down.

"Get under here," he whispered. "Stay out of sight. Don't worry. I'll take care of

you." He pushed Minsha's rump toward the space under the bottom bunk bed. It was tight, but Minsha shimmied under. She lay down as flat as she could.

Then Minsha realized she wasn't as hidden as she thought. Her tail was sticking out. And the sailor was almost there.

3

Below Deck

An old woman sat down on the bunk. She spread her long skirt over Minsha's tail.

"Thanks, Teta," Minsha heard the boy whisper.

"Teta" was what people back home called their grandmothers. Leila's teta had always slipped Minsha scraps when the other adults weren't looking.

"My family had a dog when I was a girl," the old woman whispered back.

Minsha heard stomping footsteps. She felt someone stop in front of the bunk. She could tell that it was the sailor. He smelled like sea and codfish. She held her tail as still as she could.

"What are you smiling about, old woman?" the sailor growled. "What's that? Put away your sewing until we're underway!"

Teta gasped. Minsha squirmed around

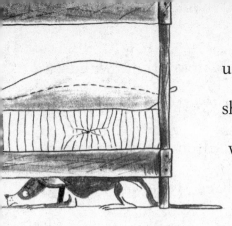

under the bunk until she could see what was going on. The sailor was trying to yank something out of Teta's hand. She was pulling back.

"Don't touch that!" Teta said. "I need it!"

"You're tearing it!" the boy named Yusef said. "Leave her alone!"

The sailor pulled harder. Not finding Minsha seemed to have put him in a bad mood. Minsha thought fast. A tower of trunks and boxes was stacked right next to the bunks.

She pushed at the bottom trunk with her head. It slid forward. *CRASH!!!* Everything that had been balanced on top of it toppled to the floor. Suddenly everyone was shouting at each other and gathering their crates and bags and boxes.

"Enough!" the sailor shouted. "Stow your belongings and keep quiet. We're about to get underway."

He stomped away.

Minsha wasn't sure if she should come out from under the bunk.

"Is your embroidery all right, Teta?" she heard Yusef ask. His voice sounded so worried! "Papa said I'm supposed to make sure you don't lose it!"

"It's just fine," Teta said.

"When they see how good your embroidery is, Teta, they'll have to let you into America!" Yusef said.

"From your mouth to God's ears!" answered Teta. "My neighbor Salma wasn't allowed to stay in America. They said she was too old and wouldn't be able to support herself. But with this I can show I can help the family earn money! I can sew and embroider for the dressmakers in America. I will be a help to you!"

"Yes, Mama," said Yusef's mother.

"Don't worry, Teta," Yusef said. "I'll take care of everything."

Teta reached her hand under the bunk. "Come on out, doggy. I can tell you are good luck for us. You saved my embroidery!"

Minsha crawled out.

"Thank you, boby," the old woman said.

Minsha wagged her tail. "Boby" was the nice word people used when talking to dogs in Syria.

"I wonder if you have a name?" Teta said.

"She has a collar," said Yusef. He looked

at it. "It says 'My name is Minsha. I belong to Leila Haddad.'

"Well, Minsha," Yusef said, "we'll see if we can find your Leila on the ship. If not, you can be in our family."

Minsha didn't know how to tell him she already had a family.

As the ship got underway, Minsha learned that Yusef was nine years old. His little sister Soussou was five. Mansour was four, Bibi was three, and Chadi was only two. Yusef said their father was waiting for them in America. He had gone the year before.

"I promised Papa I'd make sure everyone made it into America," he whispered to Minsha. "Especially Teta! I'm the oldest, so it's up to me."

Minsha had licked his hand. She understood about keeping family together.

When it got late, Yusef figured out who would sleep on each bunk.

"You can just fit here, Minsha," he said, patting one of them.

At first, though, Minsha stretched out beneath the bunk Yusef and his brothers shared. She didn't want to be seen. But she'd always slept right up next to Leila. So as soon as she heard people snoring, she crawled up to sleep between Yusef and his brothers.

"We're going to like America," Yusef whispered. "It's not like back home. In the war, people were hurt who hadn't done anything wrong. It was so unfair." Minsha

remembered how hard things had been around Mount Lebanon, with all the fighting and not enough to eat. "Things are good in America," Yusef said.

Minsha hoped so. The dog on the dock had said it would take about three weeks to get to New York City. She would be with Leila soon.

4
The Handkerchief

All through the journey, Yusef and Teta kept Minsha hidden and fed her bits of salted fish and bread they had brought with them. There was some food served on the ship. Thin soups and a few boiled potatoes and sometimes a little bit of herring. But there was never enough.

Some passengers had money to buy better food on the ship. Others, like Yusef's family, had brought extra with them. But Mama said they had to be careful not to run out, so some nights Minsha was still hungry. When that happened the man with the bunk next to Yusef's gave her biscuits and once even a piece of dried meat. He never told anyone Minsha was on board. He told Teta his name was Mr. Khoury.

Yusef asked around if there was anyone named Leila on the ship. When he couldn't find her, he seemed happy.

The ship made stops along the way. Each time they stopped, more passengers came onboard and Minsha had to be even more careful to keep hidden. One time everyone had to change to another ship. Minsha didn't know what she was going to do. But Mr. Khoury opened up his carpetbag. He took out a big coat and put it on, even though it was a warm day. With the coat gone, there was just enough room for a terrier.

"Hop in!" Mr. Khoury said. Minsha climbed inside his carpetbag. Mr. Khoury carried her to the new ship.

When they got on the new ship, she licked his face to say thank you.

He wiped his face off with a cloth.

"A journey like this makes everyone who takes it family," Mr. Khoury whispered in her big pointed ear. "We stick together."

At night, Yusef snuck Minsha out on deck to get some fresh air and let her run around. Yusef's mother never said a word about Minsha. She was always busy worrying. Worrying that one of her smaller children would get lost. Worrying that Teta wouldn't be allowed into America, even with her beautiful embroidered handkerchief. And worrying because Yusef had started coughing.

The air below deck was making a lot of people sick. It was smoky and stale. Minsha didn't mind it. It was full of interesting smells. But it was bad for the people.

"I heard that if Yusef keeps coughing the doctors at Ellis Island might think he's sick," Soussou said to her other brothers and sister. "They send sick people back."

Minsha had noticed passengers talking about that a lot. There were both inspectors and doctors at Ellis Island. The inspectors made sure people could support themselves and weren't criminals. Doctors checked everyone very carefully for any kinds of illness. If someone was sick, they might be sent back home. It was called being deported.

"Be quiet, Soussou," Yusef would say whenever she talked like that. "I'll hold it in when the doctors check me. You just be sure to do as I say when we get to Ellis Island. I'll get us all through to America."

❧

Cool air blew across Minsha's fur. She stood on deck with Yusef and his family. Other passengers crowded around them. Minsha was so excited she couldn't keep still. She kept jumping up and down and tugging on Yusef's pants leg. Ahead of them was New York City. She was almost with Leila again.

"Look!" someone shouted. "The Statue of Liberty!" Everyone aboard cheered and pointed at a giant statue of a lady holding up a torch. Teta didn't point. She was holding tight to her embroidered handkerchief. "I don't want to lose it if something happens to our luggage," she said to Yusef's mother. Mr. Khoury carefully held a large necklace made of silver coins. "I can use it to get some money

to get started in America," he told Teta. "And I speak a little English, so I can talk to people there."

Minsha paced impatiently on the deck. Finally, the ship pulled into New York Harbor.

Minsha's heart sped up in her chest. The city ahead of her looked huge. The buildings were so tall they almost reached the sky. And there were so many of them she couldn't see where they ended. It was as if giants lived there.

She would have to hurry to find Leila. Such a big city would be full of people and Leila's scent might be hard to find.

The ship pulled into the dock. The first- and second-class passengers, who had more money, got off the ship and went straight to New York City. The third-class passengers like Yusef and his family would have to go through inspection.

A sailor opened a gate. The passengers streamed off the ship and onto the dock. Minsha hurried behind Yusef, Teta, Mama, and the children. But when they followed the rest of the third-class passengers toward a smaller boat, Minsha stopped where she was on the dock. She let Yusef and his family get ahead of her.

She watched as they were pushed and pulled along with the rest of the crowd up a ramp to the boat. Yusef held Soussou's hand, and Soussou held Mansour's. Mansour held Bibi's hand. Bibi held Chadi's. Teta held Chadi's other hand. Mama carried their suitcases. They probably thought Minsha was right behind them. But she stayed on the dock and watched them until they were all safe onboard.

Goodbye, she woofed softly to their backs. She started toward the city. It was time to find Leila.

Then something caught her eye.

Teta's handkerchief. It lay on the dock. Teta must have dropped it when she was being pushed this way and that by the crowd. It was dancing in the wind, closer and closer to the water. Teta was already on the ferry. *She must be so worried,* Minsha thought.

Minsha looked toward the towering city. Leila was there. But Yusef and Teta and their family had hidden Minsha and kept her safe on the journey. She couldn't let Teta be sent back.

I can get the handkerchief to Teta

and then hop off and find Leila, she thought.

She darted to the handkerchief. She caught it in her mouth just as it was about to blow into the harbor. Then she jumped onto the small boat.

A man in uniform moved toward her. Minsha knew by now that people in uniform didn't like dogs.

She saw Mr. Khoury's big carpetbag. It was open. She jumped inside.

When the man in uniform passed by, she stuck her nose out of the bag. *Oh no!* she thought. The boat had pushed off. It was moving away from shore. Fast. She had missed her chance!

She didn't dare jump out. The man in uniform might still be nearby. She couldn't see Teta or Yusef anywhere.

A plump sparrow landed on the railing near her.

"Hey! Hey, bird!" barked Minsha. She almost lost the handkerchief, but grabbed it up again before it fell. The bird turned one eye on her.

"Dog?" the sparrow twittered. He hopped along the railing to get farther away from Minsha. "Big-eared dog!"

"Where are we?" Minsha asked.

"The Hudson River," answered the sparrow. "This boat is the ferry from New York City. All the big ships tie up at the piers here. Then the people get onto these ferryboats. They come back again later."

The sparrow spread her wings and took flight.

"But where are we going?" Minsha barked.

The sparrow's answer was a faint call on the wind. "Ellis Island!"

5

Esmeralda Delilah the Third

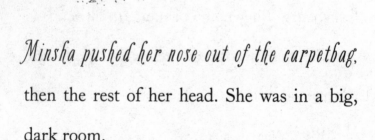

Minsha pushed her nose out of the carpetbag, then the rest of her head. She was in a big, dark room.

There was no one else in the room, but all around her were bundles and bags and suitcases and trunks. Her nose twitched. It was as if every smell of every person who had been on the ship was crammed into this one room.

She wriggled her front legs free of the bag and heaved herself out. For the first time in weeks, the floor wasn't moving beneath her paws. She felt dizzy.

Her stomach growled. Along with the smells of clothes and people, she smelled food. Cheese. She followed the scent to a lumpy bundle next to a big trunk.

She had just begun to paw open the bundle when something landed on her back. She leaped straight up into the air. Sharp claws dug into her fur.

"Get away from that!" squeaked a voice just behind Minsha's ear. A large rat clung to her back. Its tail swished in anger. "That's mine! Back away! And don't try any of that rat-catching terrier business with me! I'll chew your big ear off!"

Minsha had to fight the impulse to throw the rat off and bite her. That was what she would have done at home. But this was such a strange new place. She had no idea how things worked here.

"I'm sorry," she woofed. "I didn't know. I was just hungry."

The rat considered Minsha for a moment. Then she jumped to the floor. She landed with a soft *plop*.

"No harm done," the rat said. "No way for you to know. This is my section of the baggage room. Any food that gets left in here belongs to me."

The rat was using her tiny hands to open the bag. She tried to pull a big lump of cheese out of it. The cheese got stuck. Minsha batted at it with her paw and it fell onto the floor.

The rat gave an impressed little squeak.

"Thanks," she said. She pushed a piece of cheese toward Minsha. Minsha gobbled it down. The rat peered up at her.

"I'm Esmeralda Delilah the Third, at your service," the rat said. "I'm named after my grandmother's grandmother, who once stole an entire string of sausages from a butcher. What do they call you?"

"Minsha," Minsha said. "Where are we, exactly?"

"We're on Ellis Island," the rat said. "Otherwise known as the Island of Hope and Tears. New York is across the water on one side. New Jersey is on the other side. You can get to either one from here."

Minsha was relieved to hear that.

"Where do you want to go?" Esmeralda asked.

"New York City. That's where my family is," Minsha answered. "But first I have to find some people here." The sooner she returned Teta's handkerchief, the sooner she could find Leila. "Where do people go when they first get off the ferry?"

"The Registry Room," Esmeralda said. "You go out that door there, turn left, and across the lobby. You'll see a set of stairs. Head up those. Are those people your family too?"

Minsha hadn't thought about that. "Er . . . no."

"Then do it quick and get off the island," Esmeralda said. "If any of the officials or inspectors here see you, they'll lock you up in the pound. That's a jail for animals. Does your family know you're here?"

"No," Minsha said slowly.

"Then you'd better be careful," said Esmeralda. "If you end up in the pound, and your family doesn't come for you, you'll never get out again."

Minsha shivered.

"Thanks!" she said. "Umm . . . how would you find a family in New York? If you didn't know where to start."

"Where are your people from?" Esmeralda asked. "That might help."

Minsha thought hard for the human name for what she called home. "Syria," she woofed.

"That's easy!" said Esmeralda. "You want

Little Syria. That's where almost everyone from there goes. It's in Manhattan. On Washington Street, between Battery Park and Liberty Street."

Minsha liked Esmeralda. And the rat certainly knew a lot. She was glad she hadn't bitten her.

"How do I get there from here?" Minsha asked.

Esmeralda licked cheese dust off her paws.

"When you're done in the Registry Room, you'll see tall desks with men at them. Behind those are three doors. Behind those are three sets of stairs. Go down any one of them, turn left, and you'll see a ferry. Get on that. It'll take you to New York. But you'd better hurry—it's late, and the ferries don't run all night. When you get there, ask any mouse, rat, or pigeon where Washington Street is. Tell them Esmeralda sent you."

"They all know you?" asked Minsha. She didn't know that many animals back home!

"Of course. They're all family to me. You know how it is—family is everywhere."

Family is where Leila is, thought Minsha. She'd better hurry and get the handkerchief to Teta. And sneak onto that ferry.

"Thank you," she said to the rat. Minsha

ran back to the bag for Teta's handkerchief.

"See you around," said Esmeralda. She bit into a piece of cheese.

Suddenly Esmeralda chittered, high and sharp. Her ears twitched back and forth. "Look out, terrier!"

She scuttled between a suitcase and a bundle and disappeared.

6
Cats

Two cats strode into the room.

Minsha snorted. She knew how to handle
cats. She trotted toward them. She was careful
to keep the embroidery in her jaws.

"Out of my way," she woofed.

The cats didn't move. That had never

happened to Minsha before. The cats back home always got out of her way. Then there was a third cat in the room, and a fourth. The next thing she knew she was surrounded by them.

"Meeeeeeeeeeeowwwwwwwww," a gray

cat said. "What are you doing here, terrier?"

"This is *our* island," said a tabby. "Nothing gets done without our say-so. And we didn't say a dog could be here." He licked his lips. "We also catch all the rats."

Minsha looked to make sure Esmeralda was hidden. The rat was nowhere to be seen.

A fluffy white cat unsheathed her claws. "Hey, what's that pretty thing?" she sneered. She stretched her claws toward the cloth in Minsha's mouth. Minsha ducked.

"Leave that alone!" she barked. The handkerchief fell to the floor. She snatched it back up. She couldn't snap at the cats without losing the handkerchief again. So she growled her fiercest growl.

The fluffy cat jerked her head back. Then she pretended that she hadn't. The tabby hissed and stepped toward Minsha. The other cats followed. They closed in on her.

"What's going on here?" came a meow from near the door.

A large, sleek calico cat sat there. She was still except for a flick of her tail.

The other cats froze.

"It's Henrietta Henry," hissed the fluffy white cat.

Minsha could smell that the other cats were afraid of Henrietta.

"We found this dog, ma'am," the tabby said.

"And you didn't come get me immediately?" Henrietta meowed. She stalked over to the other cats. "You know better than that, Tiger."

Tiger the tabby flinched.

Henrietta looked Minsha over.

"I am the personal cat of the commissioner

of Ellis Island," she said. "We have rules here, and I make sure those rules are followed. No one who is sick is allowed in. No one is allowed to steal. And *no dogs* are allowed."

"I was questioning the dog for you—" Tiger said. "And there's a rat . . ."

Henrietta Henry raised the tone of her meow. "*I* make sure the rules are followed," she said. "*I* will question the dog."

No thanks! Minsha thought. The cats were so busy arguing, they'd stopped watching her. She jumped over the two cats nearest her and ran out the door toward the Registry Room.

7

The Registry Room

Minsha scurried up the staircase to the Registry Room. It was packed with people. She hoped no one would tromp on her paws.

The stairs turned one sharp corner, and then another, and then one more. At the top of the stairs, women in dark skirts and men in blue uniforms watched people climb. They pointed to the people who had trouble walking up. They pulled them aside when they got to the top. Minsha made sure to stay hidden.

Then she was in the biggest room she had ever seen.

It was as wide and long as half a dozen barns from back home put together. More people in uniforms looked down from a balcony that ran around all four sides of it. Huge windows let in the last of the afternoon light. Two big pieces of cloth with stars and stripes on them hung from the ceiling. Far away, at the other end, were the tall desks

with the inspectors standing behind them.

People from the ship lined up while doctors examined them. The doctors looked in the people's eyes and in their hair. They listened to their backs with strange gadgets made of a flat metal circle that was connected to two tubes that went into the doctors' ears.

The doctors sent most people on to talk to the inspectors. But they pulled some aside. They made marks with chalk on those people's clothes. Then men in uniform led them away.

Minsha crept forward past long, dark wooden benches that lined both sides of the huge room. There were so many people, she was afraid she'd never find Yusef and Teta. Then she heard a familiar voice.

"Soussou! Stop climbing that!"

It was Yusef!

There! He was pulling Soussou off the back of one of the benches. Mansour and Chadi ran around him in circles. They were almost at the desks where the inspectors waited! Teta clasped her hands together tightly. Her mouth was a thin, worried line.

Minsha dodged feet and bags and scrabbled under benches until she got to

Yusef. She saw him look up at Teta. "Teta, I'm so, so sorry," he said. "It's all my fault! I was supposed to take care of you!"

Teta shook her head. "No, Yusef," she said. "I was the one who dropped the handkerchief."

They both looked so miserable.

There was a gap between Yusef's pants leg and his sock. Minsha pressed her cold nose against his bare skin.

"Eeep!" Yusef said. He coughed. He looked around anxiously to see if anyone heard. It was so noisy no one seemed to. He looked down.

His mouth opened in surprise. "Minsha!"
he whispered. "We didn't know where you'd
gone!" When he knelt to talk to her, Minsha
noticed that he had a tag pinned to his coat.
A little round hole was punched through it.
Everyone else had tags pinned on their clothes
too. She'd seen dogs wearing tags but she'd

never seen people wearing them. America must be a very strange place! She had better stay out of sight, she thought. What if someone pinned a tag right through her fur!

Minsha held the handkerchief in her mouth up to Yusef.

"Oh, Minsha!" Yusef said. "You found it!" He took the bit of cloth from her. "Teta, look!"

Teta smiled in wonder. "I can't believe it!" she said.

Then it was their turn to be questioned by the inspectors. Teta walked up to the desk with Yusef's mother. Minsha stayed low, waiting for the perfect time to slip away without being seen. Teta had her handkerchief. Now Minsha could go to New York and find Leila!

The inspector spoke in a different language from Yusef's family. It must be the English Mr. Khoury had talked about. Yusef's family couldn't understand it, but another man stood next to the inspector and translated what he said.

Teta held out the handkerchief to the inspector.

"That's very nice," he said to the interpreter. "Tell her she does beautiful work. Guess she can earn her keep all right."

Teta nodded and nodded as the interpreter spoke.

The inspector asked Yusef's mother, "Is your husband waiting for you?"

"Yes," answered Mama. She was holding Mansour's hand on one side and Chadi's on the other. "He has an apartment in Little Syria."

The inspector looked at a list in front of him. He asked her more questions.

Then he said, "Do you have money with you? You have to show us that you have enough to get started in America."

Yusef's mother opened one of her bags. Inside it was a packet wrapped in paper. She unwrapped it carefully. It had another kind of paper in it.

The man nodded.

"You can all go through," the man said. "Welcome to America."

Yusef's mother and Teta both smiled. They had made it!

Minsha saw the three doors Esmeralda had told her about. She was about to run for them. Then she heard a man gasp, one desk over.

It was Mr. Khoury.

"That's not right!" she heard him say, like he couldn't believe what was happening. He was standing in front of an inspector.

And he was in trouble.

8
Thieves

Mr. Khoury was holding his big necklace made of coins. Minsha caught the glint of silver. He must have been showing that he had some-thing to sell to get started in America.

"You can give me that necklace, or I can send you back to where you came from," the inspector said very quietly. None of the

people around heard him. But Minsha could, with her sharp ears. "Hand it over, nice and low. Under this desk. Think of it as a fee for getting into America."

He can't do that! Minsha thought. *Mr.*

Khoury needs that necklace! But she knew that Mr. Khoury would do anything to be able stay in America. The inspector was stealing from someone who wouldn't dare do anything about it!

Mr. Khoury glared at the inspector. Unlike Yusef's family, he could understand him without an interpreter.

The inspector from the next desk stepped over. "Is this immigrant giving you trouble, Tom?" he said to the first inspector. Mr. Khoury held his coin necklace tight against his chest.

"He might be, Mac," Tom said. "We might need to send him back on the next ship."

Mr. Khoury gritted his teeth. But he held out the necklace to Tom. Tom looked around to make sure no one was watching. No one except Minsha!

Tom took the necklace. Mac went back to his desk. It had all happened quicker than quick.

Mr. Khoury went through to the staircases, shaking his head. Tears of rage filled his eyes.

It was so unfair! Minsha couldn't stop herself. She growled.

Yusef heard her. He looked down and then followed her gaze. He locked eyes with Tom. It was the exact moment that Tom put the necklace into his jacket pocket.

Yusef's eyes widened.

"Hey," Tom said to his friend Mac. He talked out of the side of his mouth to hide what he was saying from other people. He jerked his thumb at Yusef. "That kid saw. He'll tell somebody."

Mac was questioning someone. He looked over. He saw Yusef. Then he saw Minsha. His lips got thin and his eyes got hard.

"Not if no one is paying attention to him,

he won't," he said. He pointed at Minsha and shouted, "Who let a filthy dog in here?"

All of a sudden, everyone was looking at Minsha. Someone grabbed her by the collar. It was the inspector who had talked to Yusef's family.

"Better get this animal to the pound," he said.

Minsha couldn't let him put her in animal jail! She'd never see Leila again.

She had to get loose. She shook her whole body the way she would shake a rat she caught back home. The inspector grabbed her around the middle.

"Hey!" Yusef cried. "Leave her alone!"

He ran to the inspector and kicked him in the shin.

"Ouch!" the inspector shouted. He let go of Minsha.

"Yusef!" cried his mother. "What are you doing?!"

Minsha dove between a group of people and hid under a bench. Yusef ran back to his family.

"But, Mama!" Yusef began loudly. "He—"

Then he coughed. But this time he kept coughing and coughing and coughing.

9
Separation

The man who had been holding Minsha hurried up to Yusef. "Someone get one of the doctors," he called.

Under her bench, Minsha shook.

A woman came up to Yusef. She wore a long dark skirt and a crisp white blouse. Minsha had seen her before, at the stairs. But she hadn't realized the woman was a doctor. Most of the doctors were men.

"Dr. Rose," said Tom. "I think this boy has tuberculosis. The other doctors may have missed it."

He's trying to get Yusef sent away so no one finds out he stole the necklace! Minsha realized.

Dr. Rose frowned. She was holding one of the gadgets with the tubes and the little metal circle. She put the metal circle against Yusef's back. Then she took out a piece of chalk and put a big mark on Yusef's coat.

"No!" cried Mama and Teta together.

"His lungs don't sound good," the doctor said in English. As she spoke, an interpreter repeated what she said so Yusef's family could understand her.

"He might just have asthma, or a cold," Dr. Rose said. "But we have to make sure it's not something worse. Your son needs to have a second examination. The lung specialist has already gone home. The boy will have to stay in the hospital tonight. If he's healthy, you can come back and get him tomorrow. If he's not, he'll either have to stay here until

he's better, or go back on the next steamship."

No! Minsha thought. They couldn't take Yusef from his family.

The interpreter translated what the doctor had said. "He needs to stay with us!" Teta cried. But two men were already pulling Yusef away.

"Let go of me!" Yusef said. He kicked and struggled.

"Stop that, young man," Dr. Rose said. "Behave yourself."

Minsha could tell Yusef didn't understand. But the firm tone of the doctor's voice made him stop fighting.

"We're just taking you over there where sick people stay until we can take them to the hospital," she told Yusef. The interpreter repeated it. Minsha looked where Dr. Rose pointed. Off to the side there was a section of the room with bars around it. It looked like a big cage. There were already some people in it. People with the chalk marks that meant they were sick. Dr. Rose took Yusef's shoulder and began to lead him toward it.

"You'll be able to see him later," she said to Mama. Mama blinked back tears as she listened to the interpreter.

Some men that Minsha had heard called

"attendants" pushed Yusef's family toward the stairs.

"Yusef!" his mother cried.

Teta called, "We'll be back soon! We promise!" Teta still clutched her handkerchief, but it was no longer carefully folded. It was all balled up and crushed in her hand. Her knuckles around it were white.

Minsha didn't know what to do. She didn't want Yusef to be taken away. But she couldn't get caught, either.

"We'll take good care of him," Dr. Rose said to Mama and Teta. "Our hospital is the best . . ." She stopped talking. Her sharp eyes had found Minsha under the bench.

"Is that *a dog*?" she said.

"Yes, doctor," Tom the inspector said. "We were trying to catch it when that sick boy started coughing. Gotta get it to the pound."

They were making it all up! Minsha was furious.

"You're just trying to get Yusef and me in trouble to get away with stealing!" Minsha barked.

"We can't have an animal in the Registry Room," Dr. Rose said. "Come, dog."

She sounded just like the dogs who led the village packs back home. Minsha felt herself wanting to follow Dr. Rose's orders. She barely stopped herself from going to her.

Dr. Rose's eyes narrowed. "Dog," she said. "Behave. Attendants! Please handle this. Surely you can catch one dog."

Minsha saw three sets of boots racing toward her, then three sets of hands reaching for her.

She slid further under the bench and out from under the back of it.

Then she ran.

Behind her she heard Yusef shouting, "I thought things were fair in America!" But no one seemed to understand him.

10
The Island

Minsha bolted to the stairs and ran down them. She ended up in another room full of people.

They were pushing money across a counter and getting little pieces of paper in return. Then they took those pieces of paper, picked up their luggage, and walked out a door.

A ferryboat was waiting outside, just as Esmeralda had said. It was Minsha's way to New York City.

But will Yusef ever be able to get off the island? she thought.

Three attendants hurried down the stairs after her. They stared down at people's feet. Right at terrier level. "Find that dog," one of them said.

Minsha couldn't see anywhere to hide.

"Psst! Minsha!" a voice squeaked.

Peeking out from between two heavy trunks was Esmeralda.

Minsha scootched between the trunks.

Esmeralda's nose twitched at Minsha. "What are you doing in the railway office?" asked the rat. "I thought you had to get out of here."

Minsha told her what had happened in the Registry Room.

"Who were those men?" Minsha asked. "The ones who took Mr. Khoury's necklace?"

"Must have been Mac and Tom," the rat answered. "Stay away from those two. Most of the inspectors and doctors are good people, but those scoundrels steal from immigrants. And if they think sending you to the pound will stop them from getting caught, they'll do it. Better stay out of sight."

If Minsha got sent to the pound, she'd never see Leila again. She had to get off the island. And fast.

Yusef is probably wondering where I am, a little voice in her head said. She folded her ears against her head to block out the little voice. She had to get to Leila.

"Oh, Esmeralda!" she

said. "They're looking for me! If they catch me they'll send me to the pound! What am I going to do?"

Esmeralda fixed her jewellike eyes on Minsha.

"Well . . . can you swim?" she asked.

Minsha looked out over the water under the setting sun. Beside her, Esmeralda sniffed the air.

The two of them had hidden between the trunks until they could sneak out of the railway office unnoticed.

Now they stood on a thin strip of land that

connected the two halves of Ellis Island. The water in front of Minsha wasn't wide like the ocean. It wasn't as narrow as a stream, either, but she could see land on the other side. "That's New Jersey," Esmeralda said. "It's not too far and it's not too deep. You can get off the island that way."

"Oh," said Minsha. She wasn't as excited to hear this as she thought she would be. She couldn't stop wondering if Yusef was all right. She shook herself. Leila needed her, and Leila was in New York. "So how do I get to Little Syria from there?" she asked Esmeralda.

"Don't worry about it," said the rat. "I've got some friends who can help you out."

A flock of sparrows circled above. Esmeralda chittered up to them. They began to spiral down to land.

"Hello!" Minsha barked.

The sparrows took one look at her and scattered up into the sky.

"She's not going to eat you!" called Esmeralda. "She just wants directions!"

Minsha did the best she could to look like a dog who would never think of eating a sparrow.

The biggest sparrow flew back down and landed with his flock. Minsha recognized him. He was the sparrow who had told her the ferry was going to Ellis Island.

"Oh," he chirped. "It's the big-eared dog."

"Twitch!" Esmeralda squeaked. "This dog needs to get to her family. What's the quickest way from Jersey to Little Syria?"

"She needs to get to her flock?" twittered

Twitch. "No problem. First you cross here, then—"

"Wait," said Minsha.

Twitch and all the other sparrows stopped chirping.

"Esmeralda. Would they really send Yusef back?" Minsha asked.

"They might," Esmeralda said. "And if he's too young to go back by himself, someone in his family will have to go with him."

Minsha's chest felt tight. Just like it did when Leila's father dragged Leila away to the boat.

She looked out across the water. She knew

she could swim across and go on to find Leila.

But Yusef and Teta had worked so hard to get

to America. Now Yusef might be sent back.

Because of her.

"I can't do it, Esmeralda," Minsha said.

"Yusef helped me. I need to help him. He

needs to get back to his family too. You know

Ellis Island so well. Can you get me into the

hospital?"

Esmeralda showed her long front teeth in

a grin. "Sure thing."

11

Into the Hospital

All of a sudden the sparrows took flight.

Two attendants came around the corner of the building.

"There it is!" one of them said. "Get it! I'm not spending all night chasing a darn dog!" They charged toward Minsha and Esmeralda. One of them reached for Minsha.

Then he shouted.

"Hey! Yech! What the—?" he said.

The attendant's hands were covered with slimy white stuff. So was his friend's head. Minsha heard the laughs of the sparrows. They had pooped all over both men.

Esmeralda jumped on Minsha's shoulder.

"Go, go!" she squeaked.

Minsha went.

"Good luck!" Twitch called. The sparrows

dipped their wings and flew toward New Jersey.

❦

Minsha and Esmeralda were standing in front of a maze of buildings on the half of the island across from the Registry Room.

"Can we get in?" Minsha barked.

"Leave it to me," said Esmeralda.

She scurried around to the side of the closest building. It was made of stone with a big wooden door. The door was shut. Minsha heard a lot of whirring and clanking sounds coming through it. Right outside the door was a huge canvas bin on wheels.

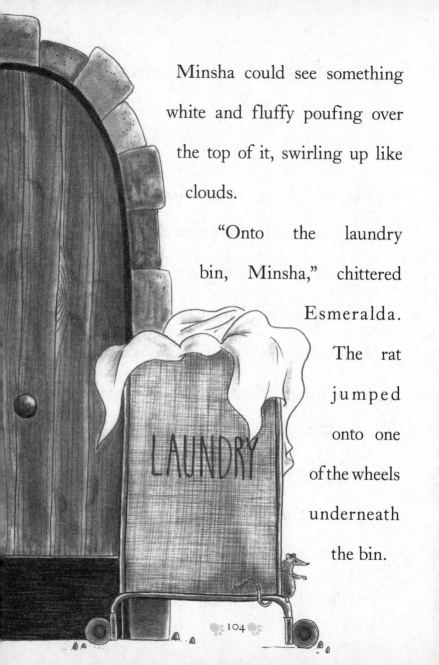

Minsha could see something white and fluffy poufing over the top of it, swirling up like clouds.

"Onto the laundry bin, Minsha," chittered Esmeralda. The rat jumped onto one of the wheels underneath the bin.

Minsha tried to climb onto the metal frame under the bin. She wriggled and squeezed. But she didn't fit.

"You'll have to jump inside," squeaked Esmeralda. "Hurry."

Two voices came from behind the building, talking and laughing. They were getting closer. Was it the men who had been chasing Minsha? No, these smelled different. Like strong soap and heat.

Minsha backed up. She took a running leap. Her back legs pushed against the earth with every bit of strength she had. She brushed the edge of the bin as she went over. She landed with a *whoosh* in a pile of whipped-up sheets. This time she made sure to tuck in her tail.

The voices reached them. Minsha held her breath.

"Gonna do a little work now, Sully? It's getting late," said one of the voices. "Or am I gonna push this laundry bin all by myself?"

"Aw, shut yer trap, Tony," said the other voice. "You couldn't push a laundry bin by yourself if it was made of feathers."

Even though their words didn't seem to

say it, it sounded to Minsha like Sully and Tony liked each other very much.

She heard the *click* of a door opening, and felt the bin being wheeled through it.

12

The Laundry Room

The room was very warm. Minsha poked her head above the sheets just enough to peer over the edge of the bin.

Huge machines churned and whirred. Young men were pulling sheets in and out of the machines. One machine made the sheets wet. Another made them dry. A dozen young men bustled around, loading and unloading and folding things.

Sully moved toward the cart. Minsha ducked down. Sully climbed up onto the railing under the bin. He started pulling out the sheets in big armfuls. Minsha dove further down into the swirl of sheets. But more and more of them disappeared from on top of her. The last one came off. The young man's eyes widened in surprise when he saw a dog looking up at him. Minsha wagged her tail.

"Hello," she woofed. It didn't help.

"Hey!" he yelled. "There's a dog in here!"

Minsha sprang from the bin onto the floor. She looked for a way out.

Sully's hands were too full to do anything about her. Some of his friends laughed.

"Friend of yours, Sully?" one of them said.

"Maybe we can keep it," another said.

But Sully shouted, "Get that dog out of here! We'll have to wash every scrap in this whole laundry again if Dr. Rose sees it! You know how she is about keeping everything clean!"

Dr. Rose! The woman who had sent Yusef to the hospital and told the men to catch Minsha. Minsha didn't want to be caught by her! She was probably one of those people who thought dogs carried germs. Dr. Rose would get her sent to the pound for sure.

Minsha saw a door opening onto a hallway. Could she get to it?

Four young men advanced on her. There were too many to dodge and they looked fast. Minsha backed away.

Esmeralda jumped out onto the floor.

"I'll take care of this!" she said. She stood tall on her back legs. "Ahem . . . *Squeaaaaaaaaaak*," she said.

"A rat!" shouted Tony. None of them paid any attention to Minsha now!

"Find Yusef! Get him out of here and back to his family!" Esmeralda squeaked to Minsha. "Don't worry about me." She winked. "I've got some tricks tucked under my ears." Esmeralda leaped straight at Sully. He jumped back. Minsha ran for the door.

The rat was off like a shot through the door too. Half the men in the laundry room raced after her.

"The hospital wards are that way! Look for rooms with lots of beds in them!" she called. She skittered in the opposite direction from Minsha. Minsha saw a long, long hallway. She headed down it at top speed.

The hallway ended. Minsha stopped running. Twilight spilled in through big glass windows. The hallway was lit with lamps, but between the lamps were patches of darkness. She could hide if anyone came after her.

She felt a pang. Where was Esmeralda? She hoped the rat was all right.

To her left was an even longer hallway. Minsha turned down it. On either side of her were doors closed tight. About halfway down the hallway, one of them was open. Through it, she saw a big kitchen that still smelled like dinner.

She probably could have found some

scraps, but she kept going. She spied another open door. She peeked around it. There were beds lined up against both walls and there were people in them. Minsha's heart raced. Maybe Yusef was there! But all the people in the room were grown-ups.

Click, clack, click. Minsha froze. Metal rattled against metal. The sound got closer and closer. *Clack, click, clack.* Minsha began to back slowly up the corridor. She sniffed the air. What kind of monster was headed straight for her? She backed up faster and faster.

Then she smelled a familiar scent. It was

as steady as a breeze on Mount Lebanon in the spring. Yusef! His scent was mixed with the scent of the metal monster. Minsha stopped backing up and ran toward the sound. Whatever the thing was, she couldn't let it get Yusef.

CLICK, CLACK, CLICK!

A metal cart came careening around the corner. That was what was making the noise! It wasn't a monster! Riding

inside the cart were a girl and two boys. One of them was Yusef!

Yusef was smiling, but his smile was sad. The other two children shook with silent laughter. It looked like they were having so much fun! Minsha ran with all her might and jumped into the cart.

"Minsha!" Yusef whispered loudly. The cart sailed down the hallway. Minsha let her tongue hang out as her ears flapped behind her. The cart went faster and faster, straight toward a wall. Yusef burst out, "Oh no!"

The cart crashed into the wall.

The kids spilled out. Books spilled out too.

Minsha tumbled tail over paws. "Minsha!" Yusef whispered, "I can't believe you're here!"

She had found Yusef! Minsha jumped up and down. She ran to him and snuffled her nose in his hand. "It's you! It's you!" she barked. Now she could help him get back to his family. She could keep him from being sent back to Syria. Then she would find Leila. She woofed again happily.

"A dog!" the other boy whispered. He spoke the same language Yusef did.

"Hello, dog," said the girl, in a different language. "Hush."

"Oh, Minsha!" Yusef whispered, petting

her head over and over. "You have to be quiet. The nurses will hear you. Then we'll all be in trouble. Come on. We'll hide you." He walked back toward the other children.

Minsha stayed where she was. She didn't want to hide. She wanted Yusef to come with her.

The girl slung an arm around Yusef's shoulder. "We have to be quiet, but do you want to go one more time?" she whispered. She pointed to the cart and pretended to climb in so Yusef would know what she meant even though he couldn't understand what she was saying.

Yusef shook his head. "No, thanks, Camila," he said. He was looking at Minsha.

"We can't be out here too long," the boy who spoke Yusef's language said. "It's almost time for the nurses to check the ward." He grinned. "I know the schedule. I know everything about the hospital. That's how I knew we could take the library book cart!"

"How long have you been here, Amal?" Yusef asked him.

"Three months," Amal said. "But some kids get sent back. That's worse. They make someone in your family go with you."

"Teta," Yusef whispered. "Teta would go. And I promised I'd make sure she made it to America." He shook his head. "I can't let Papa down."

He crouched in front of Minsha.

"You found a way in here," he said to her.

"If you got in, that means there must be a way out."

Minsha wanted to cry out, "There is! There is! The laundry room!" But all she could do was wag her tail and spin around a few times.

Yusef looked into Minsha's eyes. He spoke slowly. "Way out, Minsha? Can you show me the way out? Way out?"

Oh, honestly, Minsha thought. He didn't need to speak like that for Minsha to understand him. It must be hard to be a human and not know how to talk with other creatures. But so Yusef would understand *her*, Minsha jumped eagerly and danced on her hind legs.

"Minsha and I are getting off this island," Yusef said to the other kids.

Amal shook his head. "You'll get in so much trouble if you try to break out!" he whispered.

Camila tilted her head like she heard something. Minsha heard it too. And smelled a scent of medicine.

"Who's there?" a woman's voice said.

"It's Dr. Rose!" Amal gasped. "What's she doing here?"

13
Dr. Rose

Minsha looked for a place to hide. She spotted one of the dark patches of hallway between two lights. She grabbed the bottom of Yusef's pants with her teeth and tugged him toward it. They scooted into the dark and ducked down low. They huddled together as quietly as they could.

Dr. Rose came around the corner.

Amal and Camila didn't make it to a hiding place. The doctor frowned down at them and the overturned cart. Her back was to Minsha and Yusef.

"Camila, Amal. I'm very disappointed in you two," she said. "I was coming to check on the new boy, Yusef. I hoped you two could make him feel at home. Now just look what I find!" Minsha knew Camila and Amal couldn't understand everything Dr. Rose said. But her tone was so stern, they both looked like scolded puppies.

Minsha could feel Yusef breathing quickly. Then he coughed.

Dr. Rose jumped at the sound. Camila suddenly began to cough loud and long. In the echoing hallway, it sounded like the first cough had come from her too.

"Time to get you back into bed," Dr. Rose said to her. "And stop taking the library cart. It belongs to the school!"

She looked up and down the hallway one more time. Yusef and Minsha pressed themselves into the wall and held their breath. Dr. Rose didn't see them. She led the other two children away. Camila waved behind her back to Yusef.

When they were all gone, Minsha felt Yusef relax. But only for a minute.

"They won't tell on me," he said. "Kids stick together here. Just like home. But when they get back to the ward Dr. Rose will see the pile of pillows I left under my blanket. She'll figure out I'm gone. Oh, I'm glad to see you, Minsha!"

Yusef put his arms around Minsha for a minute. Minsha nuzzled him with her nose.

He stood up. "I know there are ferries to New York. The kids say they take the people who work here home at night. My family's going there. I know Papa lives on Washington Street."

He looked at Minsha. "It's time to get out of here, girl!"

Minsha jumped excitedly. And she felt a wave of relief. She hadn't realized how lonely it had felt trying to get to New York City by herself. Now she and Yusef could find their families together.

"Show me," said Yusef.

Minsha padded back down the hallway. Yusef followed.

But when they reached the laundry room door, it was shut.

Yusef tried the doorknob.

The door didn't budge.

Yusef rattled the door. Minsha tried to push it open with her front paws. It didn't do any good.

The laundry room was locked for the night. And Minsha didn't know any other way out of the hospital.

14
Henrietta Henry

We can't give up now, thought Minsha. Leila needed her. Teta and Soussou and Mansour and Bibi and Chadi and Mama needed Yusef.

Then Minsha saw something farther down the hallway. It was sleek and cat-shaped and had white fur on its chest. Henrietta

Henry. The cat who made sure no one broke the rules.

Henrietta was pacing slowly back and forth. She looked like she was guarding the hallway beyond the laundry room.

She's probably making sure no one sneaks out, Minsha thought. If she saw Minsha and Yusef, she'd find a way to tell someone.

And that gave Minsha an idea. Henrietta probably knew Ellis Island as well as the back of her paw. She had gotten into the hospital. Maybe she knew a way out. One that wasn't through the laundry room.

Minsha stepped out of the shadows.

The cat saw her. She hissed and arched her back. Minsha jumped and so did Yusef. Henrietta gave a little leap, then landed on all four feet. She hissed at them again.

"Scat!" said Yusef.

"Aha!" the cat meowed. "I sensed that a character of ill repute was nearby. What are you up to, dog?" She showed her sharp teeth. "What is this boy doing out here?"

Yusef stepped between Minsha and Henrietta.

Stay out of this, Yusef, thought Minsha.

He was going to ruin her plan. Minsha wished there was some way to tell him what she had in mind.

"Shoo, cat!" Yusef cried in a loud whisper. "Get away from her!" He took off his shoe and got ready to throw it. Minsha leaned against Yusef to stop him.

"Ha!" meowed Henrietta. "A dangerous character!"

"Well, then you better report us!" barked Minsha.

"I will!" Henrietta returned in an angry meow. Her eyes narrowed into amber glints. "I'm alerting the commissioner of Ellis Island immediately!"

"You do that!" Minsha barked after her.

Henrietta stalked off to the end of the hallway. Minsha followed on the cat's heels. To her

relief, Yusef came after her. He hopped on one foot as he put his shoe back on.

They reached a place where the hallway was divided in two. Just ahead, there was a window. It was open! That was how Henrietta got in!

Henrietta leaped gracefully through the open window. Minsha's plan had worked! Henrietta had shown them the way out without knowing it.

When Minsha was sure the cat was gone, she took a running leap. She jumped through the window to the ground below.

It was a tight squeeze for Yusef. He opened

the window wider. It stuck but went up a few more inches. He had to hold in his stomach and make himself as flat as he could, but he made it through. He landed on his hands and knees next to Minsha. He stood up and dusted off his pants. Minsha licked his hand, then took a deep breath. They had no time to lose.

15
The Ferry

The smell of the air and sea had never been so welcome to Minsha's nose. She could hardly keep from woofing in joy.

"We have to hurry!" Yusef whispered. "Dr. Rose must have figured out I'm gone! If we get caught now, I'll get sent back for sure!"

And I'll get locked up forever! Minsha thought.

She looked around. The laundry was to their right and a little behind them. In front of them was a big rectangle of water.

"That's where we came in," Yusef murmured, pointing across the water.

Across from them stood the Registry Room building. It was like a castle, or a city. The stones it was built with formed fancy patterns. What seemed like a hundred windows looked out toward the rest of the island.

Floating in the rectangle of water was a ferry. The boat was brightly lit. Minsha could see people heading down a paved walkway toward it.

"Amal said that that's the ferry that takes the people who work here back to Manhattan," Yusef said. "We can sneak onto it."

Minsha was thinking the same thing. She wasn't sure how they'd get on without being seen. But she and Yusef made a good team. They'd figure something out.

They ran across the narrow strip of land where Minsha had met the sparrows. Then they turned toward the big building. The ferry was filling up with people. Minsha recognized some of the workers from the laundry room.

They laughed and joked. Two young nurses chatted as they walked. Older, dignified-looking men in uniforms were stepping onto the deck.

A horn sounded on the ferry. *Hoot, hoot!*

"All aboard!" shouted a crewman.

"Come on, Minsha," Yusef said.

"Everything is going to be all right!"

Minsha was just about to make a run for the ferry when something streaked across the grass past her. It was small. It was furry. It was Esmeralda Delilah the Third. She was squeaking in fear.

Tiger, the tabby cat who had threatened Minsha in the baggage room, chased after Esmeralda. The tabby ran low and fast. Behind him was the gray cat. Behind that cat were even more cats. They squalled in rage. Esmeralda was fast but they were faster on their long, strong legs. The fluffy white cat headed Esmeralda off. Tiger pounced and landed in a crouch. He had Esmeralda!

The ferry's horn sounded again. *Hoot, hoot!*

"Now's our chance!" Yusef said. "Let's go!"

But Minsha's legs were already taking her across the grass to Esmeralda. Tiger had the rat pinned down under both front paws. The other cats had circled around.

"Get on the boat!" Minsha woofed over her shoulder to Yusef. She hoped he'd understand.

Esmeralda was fighting bravely,

scrabbling and scratching. Her skinny tail swung wildly back and forth. Tiger lowered his head. Esmeralda swatted him on the nose and almost squirmed away. Tiger calmly stepped on her again.

The cat's great jaws opened and showed his sharp teeth.

Minsha flew at the tabby. She didn't care that all the other cats surrounded her. She pawed and scratched. Tiger let go of Esmeralda to claw at Minsha. Esmeralda wriggled away!

"Run, Esmeralda!" Minsha woofed.

Tiger and two other cats jumped on

Minsha, knocking her to the ground. She scrambled and kicked. Esmeralda leaped onto the gray cat's leg. She hadn't run! But the cat shook her off. Two striped cats jumped on Minsha too. She couldn't move. She was done for.

Then something lifted a cat off her. It was Yusef. He hadn't run, either! He picked up the cats one by one and dumped them off Minsha. All the cats ran.

Yusef grinned down at Minsha. "That showed them!" he said.

But Tiger stopped running and glared back at Minsha and Yusef.

"That rat was my dinner," he said. "I'll fix you! I'm getting the boss! Henrietta Henry!" Tiger yowled. "Henrietta Henry! I found the dog! And a boy who doesn't belong here!"

He yowled and yowled and yowled. He was so loud everyone on the boat looked at him.

The fight with the cats had brought

Minsha and Yusef close to the ferry. They were standing in clear view.

"What's that child doing out?" a woman said. "And why is there a stray dog on the island?!"

Two men in uniform turned to look. Minsha froze. It was Mac and Tom. The inspectors who had stolen the silver from Mr. Khoury in the Registry Room.

"We'll take care of them," called Mac.

"Right now," said Tom.

The two thieves started toward them.

16
Enemies

Mac grabbed Yusef. Tom grabbed Minsha.

Yusef struggled.

"Stop that," Mac said. His fingers tightened on Yusef's shoulders. Minsha growled.

Mac smiled at the people on the boat.

"We'll make sure the boy gets back where he belongs," he said. "And we'll get this animal to the dogcatcher." No one but Minsha and Esmeralda could see how tightly he was holding Yusef. The people boarding the ferry turned back to the boat.

Mac and Tom are inspectors! Minsha thought. *People trust them.*

Minsha struggled too, but Tom kept a tight hold on her collar. Esmeralda squeaked and angrily puffed out her fur. The men didn't even see her. Minsha dug her claws into the grass, but Tom lifted her onto her hind legs so she couldn't get a grip. Her head bumped against his jacket. Something inside the pocket clanked. It smushed her ear. Whatever it was, it was heavy and smelled like metal.

Mac and Tom dragged Yusef and Minsha all the way past the Registry Room building. They opened a door into a smaller building next to it. It was a kitchen, but no one was in it. They took them upstairs and into a room that smelled of wood and iron. It looked like people did things with tools and lumber there.

Mac and Tom slammed the door shut behind them. They didn't see the small furry

shape slipping in just before the door closed. But Minsha did. It made her feel better to know that Esmeralda was there.

"Let go of me!" Yusef shouted even though the men couldn't understand him. "You're just trying to stop me from telling people you're thieves! You can't keep me locked up here!"

Except they can, thought Minsha.

She trembled with fury at how wrong it was. She tried to pull away from Tom. She wanted to get to Yusef. She lowered her head and twisted her shoulder. But Tom gripped her so tightly she yelped.

"Let go of my dog!" Yusef shouted.

My dog? Minsha thought.

"Shut up!" Mac hissed, putting his face right up to Yusef's. "Get that dog out of the way!" he said to Tom.

Tom opened a cupboard. He tossed Minsha inside.

"No!" Yusef shouted.

The cupboard doors closed behind Minsha with a *slam* and a *click*. She pushed up against them. Nothing happened. She was locked in.

Yusef had called her "my dog."

It was dark in the cupboard, but a little sliver of light shone through the crack between its double doors. Minsha stuck her nose right up to the crack. She could see Yusef pressed to the wall, and Tom and Mac standing in front of him.

"I told you the kid was trouble," Mac said. "He saw us take the silver earlier and now he's busted out of the hospital. He's gotta be looking for someone to tell."

Silver! That's what Minsha had felt in Tom's pocket! It was Mr. Khoury's necklace!

"Who would he tell?" Tom argued. "He

doesn't even speak English."

"I'm not willing to take that chance. You know what the commissioner will do to us if he finds out we're taking people's money," Mac said. "He says Ellis Island is supposed to be run honestly."

He took a step toward Yusef. His voice was full of menace. "We'll tell people the boy's a criminal. Then they'll deport him. That'll show him."

"No," Yusef whispered. "Deport" was the one English word just about every immigrant knew.

Minsha growled. She pushed harder against the cupboard doors. They still didn't budge.

She thought things couldn't get worse. That was when she heard Henrietta Henry meowing. First the sound came from below in the kitchen. It got stronger as Henrietta made her way upstairs.

"This way, doctor!" the cat meowed loudly. "There is a dog somewhere in this building who is breaking all the rules. I saw her going in this direction with the inspectors. This dog simply must be sent to the pound. And there is a boy with her. He is definitely not where he is supposed to be. Someone needs to do something about it . . ." The cat went on and on. She didn't seem to care if anyone could understand her. But from the  way she was yowling, even a human would know that she was telling them something was wrong.

Minsha heard the light tapping of shoes on the hard floor outside. They got closer and closer to the room.

Then a voice that scared Minsha just as much as Mac's and Tom's echoed through the hallway. "Goodness, Henrietta," Dr. Rose said. "Why are you making such a fuss? I have

a sick boy to find!"

The door to the room opened. Mac gulped. Tom's back stiffened. Yusef's eyes widened.

"What's going on in here?" Dr. Rose demanded.

17

Discovered

Minsha held perfectly still. She couldn't let Dr. Rose know she was there. Dr. Rose would send her to the pound and make sure she never saw Leila again.

There'd be no chance for Yusef now. Dr. Rose would probably make sure he left

America that instant, without even waiting for morning.

But she didn't.

"Thank goodness, Yusef!" she said. "Are you all right? I've never lost a patient before in all my time here."

Minsha could almost hear Tom puffing out his chest. "We've caught him for you, Dr. Rose," he said.

"I see that," Dr. Rose said. "But there's no reason to hold him in this room."

"He's a miscreant," Mac said. "He was running around the island looking for trouble.

We'll begin the deportation hearings as soon as possible."

"Deportation?" Dr. Rose said.

It was just as Minsha feared. They were going to send Yusef back.

No, they aren't, she thought. *Not if I can help it.* She'd thought finding Leila was the only important thing. But what good was it if she found Leila and Yusef lost his family?

We're family. We help each other, Leila had said. *We don't leave anyone behind.*

And if Mac and Tom could do this to Yusef, they could do it to anyone else they wanted, unless someone stopped them.

Family is everywhere, Esmeralda had said. Hadn't Minsha and Yusef made it all the way here on the ship together and escaped the hospital, and saved Esmeralda? *Family is even more than Yusef and Esmeralda and Teta and Mr. Khoury*, Minsha realized. It was the dog and turtle who helped her in Beirut, and Twitch, and Amal and Camila. It was every immigrant who ever walked through that Registry Room.

She had an idea. It wouldn't help her, but it could help Yusef. It could help every immigrant who would ever come to Ellis Island.

She had to show the doctor what Mac and

Tom had done! No matter what happened to her.

She barked for all she was worth. "Liars!" she woofed. "Thieves! Thieves! Thieves!"

"How on earth did that dog get in there?!" Dr. Rose said.

"I can tell you all about it, doctor," meowed Henrietta eagerly. Dr. Rose didn't pay any attention. She strode right up to the cupboard and opened it.

Minsha shot out like an arrow.

"Goodness!" cried Dr. Rose.

"Good girl, Minsha!" Yusef yelled. "Run! Save yourself!"

Minsha didn't run for the door. She aimed straight for Tom's pocket. Mac saw where she was going. He lunged for her. But right before he reached her, a furry gray shape scuttled up his arm. Esmeralda jumped on top of his head. Mac yelped and tried to grab her. Yusef shoved Mac hard. Esmeralda growled and leaped away.

Minsha wasted no time. Her sharp teeth tore Tom's pocket open with a satisfying R-I-I-I-I-P. She felt the threads snap apart.

The silver necklace spilled out onto the floor. Right in front of Dr. Rose.

Dr. Rose's voice was hard and cold.

"That is a silver coin necklace," she said. "Where would you two get something like that? No inspector on Ellis Island would be carrying that around in their pocket! You two took it from an immigrant trying to get into the country! The commissioner said that someone was stealing from immigrants. Does this boy know? Is that why you have him locked up in here?"

"Yes!" Minsha barked.

"Thief," Yusef said.

"Doctor—" Tom began.

"Quiet," said Dr. Rose. He was. Minsha was too. So was Yusef.

"I'll have you know my parents and I came to this island and walked through that Registry Room twenty-five years ago," she said. "I will under no circumstances let you send this boy away just to cover up what you've been doing. I will be reporting the two of you to the commissioner immediately."

Tom was staring at the ground. Minsha thought he might even be ashamed. But Mac was looking at Minsha. And his eyes were full of hate.

"What about that dog?" he said. "It should be locked up."

"That's for sure," Henrietta Henry meowed. She rubbed against Dr. Rose's foot.

Minsha lowered her head. She had lost her chance to find Leila. But at least Yusef would get to be with his family.

"As long as a dog stays out of my hospital and the Registry Room, she's not breaking any rules I know of," said Dr. Rose. "Especially a dog as helpful as this." She rubbed Minsha's head right between her ears.

Minsha couldn't believe it. Dr. Rose wasn't going to lock her up! Her tail wagged hard.

"So there," Minsha woofed at Mac. Then she lifted her lip at Henrietta. "So there to you, too," she said to the cat. Henrietta snarled back and slunk out of the room.

Tom and Mac eyed the door. Dr. Rose stepped in front of it. Minsha did too.

"Don't even think about it," Dr. Rose said.

"You heard her!" squeaked a voice at Minsha's paw. Esmeralda Delilah the Third squinted up at Minsha.

"Is that a rat?" Dr. Rose said.

"Oops! See you later," said Esmeralda, dashing out the door. She looked over her shoulder once.

Family is everywhere, her toothy grin seemed to say.

18
The Kissing Post

The next morning Yusef and Minsha ran past the kissing post down the stairs from the Registry Room. Families who had been apart for a long time hugged and kissed when they saw each other there. Yusef's father, a big man with eyes like Yusef's, was holding his arms wide. Yusef ran to him and his father hugged him tight. The whole family had come to get him.

"Don't forget Minsha!" called Yusef. His father picked her up and hugged her too. He smelled like Yusef. Minsha licked his face to say hello.

The night before, Dr. Rose and the commissioner of Ellis Island had Mac and Tom arrested. And it turned out the commissioner liked dogs. Minsha spent the night on a blanket on his kitchen floor. Henrietta Henry didn't like it at all. But she stuck to walking by Minsha every few minutes and giving her suspicious stares.

Dr. Rose herself had made sure the lung specialist saw Yusef first thing that morning. He said Yusef did not have tuberculosis and could leave Ellis Island for the city. He did say that Yusef had something called a respiratory infection from the bad air below decks on the ship. Yusef's family used  some of their precious money to pay for medicine so it didn't get worse and turn into something called pneumonia.

"Now, you take all that medicine, young man," Dr. Rose said. "Or I'll want to know why."

When the interpreter repeated what Dr. Rose said, Yusef's eyes got wide. He nodded.

The commissioner had something to say too. He came to the kissing post to shake Yusef's father's hand.

"We've suspected someone was taking

things from immigrants for some time," he said. The interpreter repeated it. "But we weren't able to catch the thieves. Now we have. Justice is restored on Ellis Island because of this boy." Minsha stood proudly at Yusef's side. "And of course," added the commissioner, "because of this dog."

He shook Yusef's hand. When Minsha held up her paw, he shook it too.

"I think there are good people and bad people everywhere, Minsha," Yusef said into her ear. Minsha thought so too.

Minsha knew Yusef would be well. And he and Teta and Mama and Soussou and Chadi and Bibi and Mansour were all together again.

But even though she was happy for them, she felt like there was a big emptiness inside her. Would she ever see Leila again, she wondered?

Epilogue

Little Syria, New York City

Minsha trotted beside Yusef through the busy streets of Little Syria. Yusef was carrying bread from the bakery home to his mother. That was his job.

The bread was warm from the oven. The scent of it rose from the napkin it was wrapped in. It smelled delicious. Minsha's mouth watered.

They had been in Little Syria for two weeks. Yusef was much better. Teta and Yusef's mother were already doing work sewing. They worked from the first morning light until the sun went down. Yusef's father sold tea throughout the neighborhood. He walked around with a huge shining tea urn strapped to his back. Teta always came outside for a few minutes at lunchtime to have some tea.

Minsha stuck close to Yusef. Esmeralda had been right. Somehow, Yusef had become part of her family. So had Esmeralda, and Mr.

Khoury. But a part of her was sad. She missed Leila. She had looked and looked for her when she arrived in Little Syria. But there were so many people and smells that she hadn't been able to find her.

"There's Baba and Teta!" cried Yusef. He ran to his father and Teta and kissed them both. Minsha sniffed at Teta's embroidered handkerchief. Teta always kept it tucked in her apron.

"Break me off some bread, Yusef," his father said. He smiled as he chewed the warm bread. Minsha sat at his feet, hoping he'd drop some crumbs.

Then she heard a girl's voice.

"What a pretty handkerchief," the girl said. "Look at all the colors."

Minsha's big ears twitched. Her nose sniffed and sniffed. Her tail waved. She would know that voice and that scent any-where. She was on her hind legs barking before she knew it.

"Leila! Leila!"

The girl whipped around. Her mouth dropped open.

"Minsha!" she shouted.

Minsha hurled herself at Leila. Leila held out her arms. Minsha leaped into them, accidentally knocking Leila to the ground. Leila laughed. Minsha couldn't stop wriggling and licking Leila's face.

"I can't believe you're here!" Leila cried. "How did you get here?"

With Yusef's help, Minsha wanted to say.

She stopped wriggling. She suddenly wasn't sure what to do.

Yusef walked over to Minsha and Leila.

"She knows you," Yusef said slowly.

Leila nodded. "See her collar? Leila Haddad. That's me."

"So . . . she's your dog," Yusef said. He sounded sad. "Well, she's the best dog in the world."

"I know," said Leila.

Minsha wanted to cry. She wanted both Leila and Yusef!

"You're very lucky to have such a wonderful dog," said Yusef. "We've been through a lot together. You better take her home with you, since she's yours."

He sniffled.

Leila looked at him a long time. She held out her hand. "We both live in Little Syria. Maybe Minsha can be your family's dog *and* my family's dog together," she said.

Yusef took her hand.

"I'd like that," he said. "She can be in both of our families."

"Everyone here needs to be family," Leila said.

Minsha jumped joyfully from Leila to Yusef and back again. They petted her head while they talked.

"Well, look who's here!" said a voice behind them. They all looked up. Mr. Khoury was wheeling a small cart full of vegetables through the street. "Look at what I used the money from the silver necklace for, Yusef! My start in America! Thanks to you and Minsha here!"

With a wave to them, he went on up the street.

The scents and sounds of Minsha's new home danced around her nose and ears. She looked from Yusef to Leila, and at all the people on the busy streets. Her new family.

Authors' Note

Ellis Island

Over twelve million people came through Ellis Island from the time it opened in 1892 until the day it closed in 1954. Forty percent of the people in the United States are descended from these immigrants. They came from all over the world.

Many of them were children, including the first people who came to America through Ellis Island. Fifteen-year-old Annie Moore from Ireland was the very first. She came with her two brothers, Anthony and Phillip, who were eleven and seven years old. The commissioner (the person in charge of Ellis Island) gave her a gold piece worth ten dollars. If you go to Ellis Island, you can see a statue of Annie and her brothers.

Usually children came with their parents, but sometimes they came alone. Some were meeting family members. Others were orphans. They were taken care of on the island until immigrant aid societies or sponsors could find homes for them. There was a school on Ellis Island and a playground. And, for a time, a library book cart like the one in our story.

People came to Ellis Island for many different reasons. Many came to the United States to escape wars or poverty, or because there wasn't enough food where they lived. Others came to join family members who had arrived before them, or for jobs.

Coauthor Pam Berkman's grandfather

entered America through Ellis Island in 1919. Here is a photo of the ship he journeyed there on.

How Did People Get to Ellis Island and What Happened Once They Got There?

People came to Ellis Island on ships from

ports in Europe, the Middle East, Africa, and the Caribbean. Once the steamship was invented it took about two to four weeks to make the journey across the Atlantic Ocean. Before immigrants even got on the ships, they had to prove they were healthy and had some place to go in America. Then, when the ship got to New York Harbor, officials boarded it to make sure there were no diseases, like cholera, among the passengers. If the ship was safe, it was allowed to dock in New York along the Hudson River. Passengers who rode in the first- and second-class parts of the ship went through the immigration process onboard. They could then get off and go wherever they wanted. Passengers with less money who rode in the third-class part of the ship had to get on another boat. That boat took them to Ellis Island.

Once they were there, they had to go through two kinds of inspection. First, doctors checked them to make sure they weren't sick—the doctors wanted to make sure they weren't bringing contagious diseases to America. They also wanted to make sure the immigrants were strong enough to work and would not have to be taken care of. The doctors saw thousands of immigrants each day, and had to work quickly. They were so fast that their inspection was called the "six-second physical."

If an immigrant passed the medical inspection, they would then talk to an inspector, who might also be called an interrogator. That inspector would ask them questions about where they came from and what they were going to do in America. They asked questions to make sure the immigrants' answers matched what was on the ship's manifest, the list of who was onboard. They checked that the immigrants had somewhere to go and enough money to get started.

Because many of the immigrants didn't speak English, interpreters helped them understand what the inspectors were saying.

Almost all immigrants made it through the inspections. Some did not. If the inspectors thought the person was a criminal or couldn't support themselves, or had nowhere to go, they would send them home. If the doctors thought the immigrant was sick, they would send them to the hospital. The hospital on Ellis Island was one of the most modern in the world. It used the methods Florence Nightingale had invented to make sure germs didn't spread. Sometimes people stayed just overnight. Sometimes they stayed for months. And sometimes they were sent back home. Families could be separated, which is one of the reasons Ellis Island was called "the Island of Hope and Tears."

Not All Americans Are Immigrants

Not everyone who lives in the United States came through Ellis Island. Some immigrants came through places like Angel Island in California or landed in America before or after Ellis Island was used. But not all Americans descended from immigrants. When the

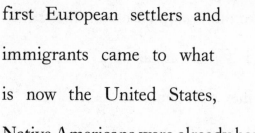

first European settlers and immigrants came to what is now the United States, Native Americans were already here. Then, during slavery, people from Africa were kidnapped and brought over in slave ships.

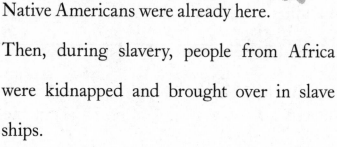

Our Story

Yusef and his family come from what is now called Lebanon. Back in 1921, when *Minsha's Night on Ellis Island* is set, it was called Greater Syria. Like millions of people before and after them, Yusef's family came to find a better life. In our story, Yusef and his family came to escape the hunger and poverty that resulted from war.

Corruption on Ellis Island

Most people who worked on Ellis Island were honest, and were truly concerned about the immigrants. We made up the characters of Mac and Tom, but there was also corruption on Ellis Island. Usually it was officials who took bribes to let people skip inspection, or to get through if they were sick. But sometimes inspectors would demand money to let people through. Other people who worked at Ellis

Island, like baggage handlers, sometimes cheated immigrants.

Dr. Rose

We made up Dr. Rose. But she is based on two of the first women doctors on Ellis Island. They were Rose Bebb and Rose Faughnan. For a long time, only men were doctors on Ellis Island. Dr. Bebb was the first female doctor, and she was hired in 1914.

Acknowledgments

When we got the idea for At the Heels of History, we could only have dreamed of working with a team as skilled and supportive as the one at Margaret K. McElderry Books. Heartfelt thanks to the wonderful Nicole Fiorica, whose sharp insights and editorial guidance made Minsha's story so much stronger. Thank you to Ruta Rimas for bringing At the Heels of History to McElderry and for her editorial guidance on the first two books of the series. Thank you to publicist Milena Giunco, and to Barbara Fisch and Sarah Shealy at Blue Slip Media for helping us share the doggos with the world.

Thank you to illustrator Claire Powell for her beautiful renderings of Minsha and her world. We could not have hoped for a better illustration of our story.

A million thanks to the always brilliant, encouraging, and insightful Mollie Glick and the team at CAA.

Thank you to Nora Boustany, journalist

and lecturer at the American University of Beirut, for her cultural review of *Minsha's Night on Ellis Island*, her insights and guidance on life in Lebanon and the lives of Lebanese immigrants, and on so many details of names and culture—and thank you to Heather Bourbeau for introducing us to Nora. Thank you to Barry Moreno, librarian and historian at the Statue of Liberty National Monument and Ellis Island Immigration Museum, for talking to us for an hour when we arrived unannounced at the Ellis Island library, reviewing the manuscript for us, and giving us his time to answer our questions via phone and email. Thank you to George Tselos, supervisory archivist at the National Park Service, for sharing his wisdom about Ellis Island and US immigration. Thank you to Patrick Montiary, public programs manager at Save Ellis Island, for the tour of the abandoned Ellis Island hospital and for insights into the lives of the immigrants who stayed there. Thank you to Lorie Conway, director of the amazing film *Forgotten Ellis Island* and author of the book by the same name, for her help answering our detailed questions on Ellis Island.

We are indebted to the expertise of all of these people. All errors are our own.

Thank you to the Berkeley Public Library and Contra Costa County Library for the access to every book we could possibly need.

We could not have written this book without the guidance and support of our writing partners: Lucy Jane Bledsoe, Michelle Hackel, Mary Mackey, Lisa Riddiough, and Elizabeth Stark. Thank you to Debbie Notkin for helping us successfully navigate the world of coauthoring a creative project.

Pam would like to thank Max and

Caspian for their patience and understanding while Mom was busy writing, and her husband, Mehran, and sister, Brenna, for their support and love. Dorothy would like to thank her family and friends for their love, encouragement, and support. None of this happens without all of you. Thank you to the Writers Grotto and Word of Mouth Bay Area. And, of course, thank you to dogs. You're all very good dogs.